KEELEY: BOOK FOUR
KEELEY
CARRIES ON
DEBORAH ELLIS

**Look for the other Keeley stories
in Our Canadian Girl**

Book One: The Girl from Turtle Mountain

Book Two: Keeley's Big Story

Book Three: Keeley and the Mountain

KEELEY: BOOK FOUR

KEELEY
CARRIES ON
DEBORAH ELLIS

PENGUIN
CANADA

PENGUIN CANADA

Published by the Penguin Group

Penguin Group (Canada), 90 Eglinton Avenue East, Suite 700, Toronto, Ontario, Canada M4P 2Y3
(a division of Pearson Canada Inc.)

Penguin Group (USA) Inc., 375 Hudson Street, New York, New York 10014, U.S.A.
Penguin Books Ltd, 80 Strand, London WC2R 0RL, England
Penguin Ireland, 25 St Stephen's Green, Dublin 2, Ireland (a division of Penguin Books Ltd)
Penguin Group (Australia), 250 Camberwell Road, Camberwell, Victoria 3124, Australia
(a division of Pearson Australia Group Pty Ltd)
Penguin Books India Pvt Ltd, 11 Community Centre, Panchsheel Park, New Delhi – 110 017, India
Penguin Group (NZ), 67 Apollo Drive, Rosedale, North Shore 0632, New Zealand
(a division of Pearson New Zealand Ltd)
Penguin Books (South Africa) (Pty) Ltd, 24 Sturdee Avenue, Rosebank, Johannesburg 2196,
South Africa

Penguin Books Ltd, Registered Offices: 80 Strand, London WC2R 0RL, England

First published 2007

1 2 3 4 5 6 7 8 9 10 (WEB)

Manufactured in Canada.

Library and Archives Canada Cataloguing in Publication data available upon request.

ISBN-13: 978-0-14-305155-8
ISBN-10: 0-14-305155-5

Visit the Penguin Group (Canada) website at **www.penguin.ca**

Special and corporate bulk purchase rates available; please see
www.penguin.ca/corporatesales or call 1-800-810-3104, ext. 477 or 474

To Connie, Adam, Marcus, and Katie

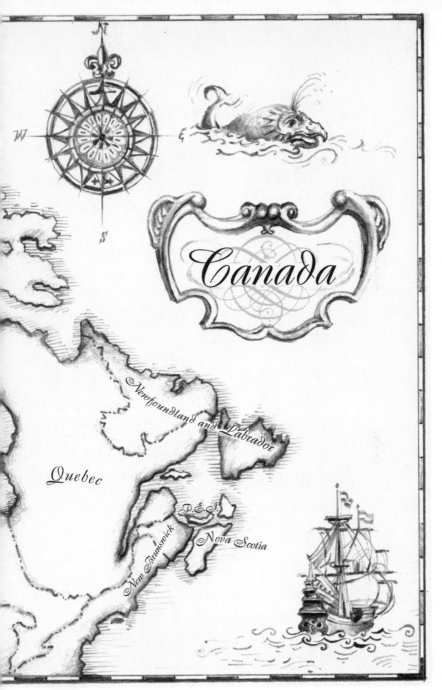

Canada

Quebec

Newfoundland and Labrador

P.E.I.

New Brunswick

Nova Scotia

 Marks the location of the story

KEELEY'S ADVENTURE CONTINUES

TEN-YEAR-OLD KEELEY O'BRIEN IS SUDDENLY FACING a very different life. She had been living in the coal-mining town of Frank, Alberta, deep in the Crowsnest Pass of the Rocky Mountains. There she went to school, worked at the newspaper, and got herself in and out of trouble. She was very happy, staying at the boarding house with her father and watching as the town grew around her. That was until April 29, 1903, when a huge chunk of rock slid off Turtle Mountain and buried much of the town. About seventy people died that day, including Keeley's father. Keeley became an orphan.

Keeley's strict grandmother swooped into town to take charge. She decided that Keeley was growing up a little too wild from years of running free in the Western wilderness among people with big dreams and rough manners. Keeley was bundled into a train and taken away to live in quiet, refined Lethbridge, where her grandmother could turn her into a lady.

But Keeley has other plans. Her work at the local newspaper and a meeting with Cora Hind, the famous reporter, makes her want a bigger life than her grandmother has in mind for her. Will she have the courage to go after it?

CHAPTER Nᵒ 1

"*Coming into Winnipeg! Winnipeg, next* stop!"

The train conductor's bellow woke Keeley out of the sleep she'd finally been able to slide into. The floor of a railway car was not a comfortable spot, particularly when she was also trying not to be noticed. Her whole body was stiff and sore.

Around her, the other passengers started stirring. Some had been awake and talking since daybreak, excited about arriving. Others opened one eye, grunted, then tried to go back to sleep. They were going on to Toronto and had a long way to go yet. The more of the journey they could sleep through, the faster it would go by.

Keeley felt around her, to make sure she still had her bundle. She also checked her jacket pocket for the five dollars she'd tucked away, her prize from the spelling bee back in Frank, Alberta. Her money was still there.

She pushed thoughts of her town from her mind. She had too many other things to worry about right now. She couldn't afford to be sad.

The train lurched, and Keeley reached out to steady herself.

"Hey! Watch what you're grabbing!"

A small, angry boy yanked his foot out of Keeley's hand.

"Why are you on the floor?" he asked, kicking at her head. "Mama! There's a girl on the floor and she hurt me!"

"I didn't hurt him," Keeley said. *Although I will if you don't shut up*, she thought.

"What are you doing down there, little girl?" the mother asked.

"My mother needed room for the baby," Keeley lied.

"Well, go back to her now."

Keeley tried to get to her feet. One leg was asleep, and she had to endure a few more kicks to her head before stumbling out in the aisle. She wished there were someone she could brag to about being so mature and not slugging the annoying boy. But there was no one.

Keeley's mother, a painter, had died when Keeley was seven, four years ago. After two dreadful years with her old, stuffy grandparents in Lethbridge, Keeley and her father moved to Frank, a new town in the Crowsnest Pass in the Rocky Mountains. They had been very happy there. Her father worked in the mine. Keeley had friends and enemies, things she loved and hated, people to care for and people to annoy—all the things that make up a good life.

And then, like the mountain, it had all come crashing down.

The next thing Keeley had to worry about now was getting safely off the train. She didn't have a ticket. She'd meant to buy one in Lethbridge after slipping away from her grandmother, who was taking her toward a life of doilies and good behaviour. But the train to Winnipeg was pulling away from the station. She had to act fast.

So far, she'd managed to avoid the ticket-takers by moving around, hanging out with families, and pretending to be asleep. If she could just get off the train, she'd be home free.

Except that she wouldn't be home.

"Can I help you?" she asked the woman in front of her in the aisle.

"Oh, that would be so kind!" The woman was struggling with too many parcels and too many children. Her husband stood with his back to them. What he didn't see, he didn't have to help with.

Keeley picked up one of the squirming creatures. The ticket-taker, if there was one when she left the train, would think she was part of this family.

"Thank you," the woman said. "Someone is meeting you?"

"That's right," Keeley told her.

Keeley had told so many lies on this trip, she had lost count. Lies had gotten her food, places to sit, and shelter from the ticket-takers. There was no point in feeling good or bad about it. That's just the way it was.

The train slowed down, finally coming to a stop. It took a long time to empty out. Some people waited for the train to stop before getting out of their seats, then blocked the aisle for everyone else as they gathered their belongings. The child in Keeley's arms fussed and grew heavy.

Bit by bit, Keeley moved through the train. When she got to the door, the porter at the bottom of the steps took the child from her arms and helped her out of the train. He didn't ask her for a ticket.

Keeley walked quickly down the platform and into the Winnipeg train station. The next stage of her life was about to begin.

Whatever that would be.

CHAPTER N° 2

Keeley's stomach was growling so much she was sure it could be heard over the many voices in the train station.

She'd had a few things to eat on the train, but not nearly enough. Before going out into the city, she needed to eat.

Keeley curled her fingers around her money. She could smell something delicious on the other side of the station.

The big, open space of the station was packed with people. Keeley headed into the crowd. They were all men, and they weren't moving.

Keeley, more hungry than curious, kept pushing her way through. Adults were strange creatures anyway—most of what they did made no sense to her.

"Excuse me, pardon me," she mumbled as she moved in between the men. Then, all of a sudden, there were no more.

Keeley found herself facing a different group of men, who were staring at the men in the line she now stood with.

This other group of men, looking tired, ragged, and confused, stared back at Keeley and the men on her side. A man in a suit got between the two groups and started talking.

"Most of you farmers have done this before. We'll do it the same as last year. Here are the farm hands. Look 'em over. If you see someone you like, offer him a job."

"This is a skinnier-looking group than last year," one of the men on Keeley's side of the room yelled. "Don't they have any real men back in the East?"

"Work 'em awhile. They'll get some muscles."

"Maybe if they fed us on the train, we wouldn't look so skinny," one of the men looking for work shouted.

"Work first, then eat," the farmer shouted back. "We're not rich people either."

"All right, all right, let's get this done," the man in the suit said. "Anyone who isn't chosen goes back on the next train. Winnipeg has enough unemployed men."

The farmers from Keeley's side of the room walked over to the men on the other side. Keeley walked with them, moving closer to the food smells. She could hear their conversations.

"You're not afraid of hard work, are you?"

"You're not afraid to pay me, are you?" was the answer. "Last year the man I worked for deducted so much for my room and food, there was nothing left for my family."

"We're not all like that," the farmer said.

"That one's a troublemaker," Keeley heard someone say. "Send him back to Toronto."

"I need to work!" the man yelled.

Keeley was too hungry to hang around to see what would happen next. Instead she followed her nose to the food stand in the corner.

"I'm hungry," she told the woman behind the stand.

"You've come to the right place, if you have money," the woman answered.

"I have money," Keeley said, taking her five dollars out of her pocket. "What smells so good?"

"Cornish pasties," the woman said. "My own recipe, brought over from England. Beef and potatoes and carrots all baked in pastry. I keep them hot with the coals in my cart."

"I'll take one," Keeley said.

"Fine," said the woman. "Where's your mother? Is it all right with her for you to be spending that money?"

"My mother's dead."

"What about your father?"

"He's dead, too. I'm from Frank. My father was killed by Turtle Mountain."

"Oh, you poor child," said the woman. "It was in all the papers. Such a terrible thing to happen."

Forget the sympathy, Keeley thought. *Give me the food*.

"Who are you travelling with?"

"I'm on my own."

"Is somebody meeting you?"

"No." Keeley pushed the money at the woman. She looked up at her, then realized she'd made a mistake. "I mean, yes, my aunt is meeting me."

Keeley was an experienced enough liar to know she'd just blown it.

"I'm really hungry!" Keeley said, her voice rising.

The woman waved someone over. A policeman was soon at Keeley's side.

"Who have we here?" The policeman looked down at Keeley.

"Another runaway," the food woman said.

"A very young one," the policeman said. "You'd better come with me."

"I haven't done anything wrong!" Keeley protested.

"And we'd like to keep it that way," the officer said, taking her arm. "Winnipeg is not the place for a child alone."

Keeley had just enough time to grab her money off the counter.

The crowd of farmers and workers parted for Keeley and the policeman. Keeley kept her eyes on the ground. She hadn't done anything wrong, but still she felt ashamed. All these people would think she was a thief, or worse!

"Take care of yourself, kid," someone said. Keeley looked up. The man who had been called a troublemaker put a hand on her shoulder as she walked by.

"You wouldn't be interfering with police business, would you?" the officer asked him.

"Just wishing the little lady well," the man replied.

"We're not thugs," said the policeman. "She'll be safer with us."

Keeley's resolve not to cry broke down, and she sobbed all the way to the police station.

At least they fed her.

"You can share my lunch," the policeman said as he led her to a chair near his desk. "My wife always packs me a lot of food."

Keeley quickly devoured a cold meatloaf sandwich. It wasn't a Cornish pasty, but it was pretty good. She was so hungry that the policeman's hat would have been delicious. After the sandwich came an apple and a raisin cookie. She washed it all down with a drink of water.

No longer hungry, Keeley could turn her attention to other things.

"Are you going to put me in jail?" she asked the policeman. He was busy with some papers, and she had to ask him twice before he answered.

"We'll find a place for you," he replied. "You just sit tight until someone has time for you."

It wasn't much of an answer, but at least he didn't seem in a hurry to lock her up.

Sitting in the police station was almost as interesting at standing at the saloon window with her friend Patricia back in Frank, watching the drunks get into fights.

Thinking of Patricia made her homesick for her town, and that made her miss her father, and that made her want to cry again. She made herself stop thinking of home, and just sat and watched.

Men in suits and uniforms walked back and forth, looking important. A man was brought in who had too much to drink. Keeley watched him being taken into a room at the back. She could see bars on the cells back there.

The policeman sat back down at his desk. "All right, young lady, now we'll see what we can do for you. Tell me your name and where you come from, and don't waste my time with any fibs."

Keeley hadn't yet gotten a story together in her mind. She wasn't about to tell him the truth and be sent right back to Lethbridge. As she looked around for a way to stall, there was a commotion at the door, and several policeman brought in a man who was struggling and shouting.

"It's not fair!" he shouted. "It's not right! Human beings should not be treated like this!"

Keeley recognized him—he was the trouble-maker from the train station.

Keeley's cop went over to help the others.

"Disturbing the peace," Keeley heard, and "Resisting arrest," and "Assaulting a police officer."

"I just want a job!" the man shouted. "I have children back east. You bring us out here, you don't feed us, and you want me to just leave, like it doesn't matter? Like my children don't matter?"

His voice faded away as he was taken into the back room. Keeley heard the steel door bang shut. She could hear the man sobbing inside his cell.

Without thinking much about it, Keeley slipped the rest of the cop's lunch off his desk. The policemen were all busy discussing what had happened. Quickly, she stepped into the back room. The crying man was in the centre cell.

"Here," she whispered. "Take this. It's pretty good." The sandwich had to be squished a bit to fit through the bars, but that wouldn't affect its taste.

The man looked up, wiped his tears, and grabbed the food. From the way the sandwich disappeared, Keeley could tell he was as hungry as she had been.

"The police are working men, just like me," he said, his mouth full of meatloaf. "Why do they come down so hard on a man who's just like them, who just wants to feed his family?"

"Here," she whispered. "Take this. It's pretty good."

Keeley didn't have an answer. She didn't think he really expected her to.

The food calmed him down. "Are you OK?" he asked her.

"I don't know," she answered. "I don't know what they're going to do with me."

"We'll put you in a cell if you come back here again," her policeman said, suddenly appearing in the doorway. "Get out of there. These men deserve some privacy. They're not to be gawked at like animals in a zoo."

"I wasn't gawking," Keeley said. She just had time to raise her hand in a wave before she was taken out and put back in the chair.

"Stay there. I'll be right back."

This was her last chance. Holding tightly to her bundle, Keeley ran for the door. She reached the sidewalk and kept running, turning corners and zipping down alleys, not looking back to see if she was being followed.

She kept running until her legs ached. It started to rain, so she ducked into a doorway. The door was open, and since the rain was coming down hard enough that she was still getting wet, she went inside, climbing the staircase just inside the door. No one was around.

The staircase led to a big room with very dim lights. Keeley spotted a sofa with a blanket across the back.

Weariness caught up with her. Using her bundle as a pillow, Keeley wrapped herself in the blanket, curled up on the sofa, and fell into a deep sleep.

CHAPTER N.º 4

"*Oh, my darling Jezabel. If only we could* be together like this always."

"Heathcliffe, dearest, we must not hope for things that cannot be."

What in the world was going on? Sleep left Keeley's brain. She heard two people talking, but what they were saying was completely silly.

Keeley pulled the blanket off her head and blinked at the row of bright lights in front of her.

"Oh, my little buttercup. No one must know our secret!"

Two people in fancy clothes were sitting at a

small table a little bit in front of Keeley. She swung her feet to the floor and raised her hand to her eyes to shelter out the bright lights so she could see where she was.

Keeley heard laughter coming from beyond the lights. The laughter grew as she stood up and took a few steps.

"Jezabel, sweetness, at least for this moment we are all alone!"

The laughter rose in a wave. The woman at the table turned her head, saw Keeley, and screeched.

I can't look *that* bad, Keeley thought, smoothing down her hair. One of her braids had come undone.

"Get off the stage!" the man and woman at the table hissed at her, making shooing-away movements with their hands while still trying to be lovey-dovey with each other for the audience.

Keeley looked around to see which way to go. She tried to leave through the curtains at the back but couldn't find the opening. She ran to one side, then switched directions and ran to the other. Both sides had angry-looking men ready to grab her.

The best route for escape seemed to be straight ahead.

Keeley could see the heads of the audience below the stage, but there wasn't time to look for steps.

I'll have to jump, she thought. If she sat on the edge of the stage, then jumped to the floor, it wouldn't be that far.

Just a few more steps, and she'd be at the edge. Everything was happening very quickly.

She was almost there when she tripped over an uneven board on the stage floor. She tumbled forward, her arms flailing about trying to grab onto anything that would steady her.

Her hand came down on the man actor's head. She heard him bellow, and, as she continued her tumble downward, she heard the audience roar with laughter.

Keeley hopped to the floor and ran toward the doors at the back. She felt something in her hand and lifted it up to see. It was the actor's wig.

Why do grown-ups wear fake hair? She flung the wig away, pumped her legs faster, and pushed through the doors onto the street.

"I'm safe!" she exclaimed.

Now what? It would soon be nighttime. She was hungry again, and no closer to doing what she had come to Winnipeg to do.

With no choice but to walk, Keeley walked.

"Hey, kid. Are you lost?"

A man standing against the side of a building held out his hand to stop her.

"I'm not really sure."

"It's going to be dark soon," he said. "You don't want to be out wandering around the city after dark. It's dangerous."

"I don't know where to go," Keeley told him.

The man smiled. "Why don't you come with

me? We could have some supper, and I have a spare room you can sleep in."

"That's awfully kind of you," Keeley said.

"People are supposed to be kind to each other. Don't you agree?"

Keeley did agree.

The man held out his hand to her again. She reached out to take it, then felt herself pulled away.

"What do you think you are doing?" An angry woman came between Keeley and the man. "Frankie, get out of here, or I'll start hollering for the cops."

"You don't want the cops any more than I do." Frankie's smile turned into a sneer.

"I'll take my chances. Beat it."

Frankie slunk away.

The woman turned her anger on Keeley. "Were you born yesterday?" she yelled.

"I don't understand—" Keeley began.

"You're too stupid to be out alone," the woman said. "You clear off, too. If you're killed, the cops will come swarming, and nobody needs that."

"But I don't know where to go!" Keeley didn't want to start crying again, but she was afraid she was getting close.

The woman's face softened a little. "Runaway?"

Keeley nodded. That's really what she was.

"Got any money?"

"Five dollars."

"So you're not entirely stupid. Go two blocks that way." She pointed down the street. "There's a boarding house, the Grand Arms. Don't flash your money around. Stay there tonight. Tomorrow, do us all a favour and go back to where you came from."

She pushed Keeley away. Keeley wanted to say thank you, but the woman had turned her back.

Keeley walked to the boarding house. She was looking forward to a hot meal and a clean bed. She was used to boarding houses. Everything would be all right.

The Grand Arms looked like a stiff wind would blow it away. The grey steps up to the front door were covered in muddy footprints.

There had been mud in Frank, too, but Mrs. Greer's steps had been clean.

Keeley knocked on the door. When no one answered, she opened it, and timidly stuck her head inside.

"What do you want?"

Keeley couldn't tell if the raspy voice belonged to a woman or a man. She took a few steps inside. It took a moment for her eyes to adjust to the dimness.

"I'd like a place to sleep."

"One night?"

The voice was coming from the other side of a high counter.

"I think so. How much do you charge?"

A knobbly hand appeared on the counter, tapping a piece of paper there. Keeley stood on her tiptoes to read it. A deluxe bed was one dollar a night. An ordinary bed was fifty cents.

"An ordinary bed, I guess," she said. "And supper."

Keeley put her money on the counter, received her change, and was told to go to room four. "Get your supper in an hour."

Keeley was all set with an explanation of why she was on her own, but the raspy voice didn't ask her. Keeley didn't mind rudeness, but it made her lonely to realize that the raspy voice just didn't care.

Supper was a plate of baked beans and a hunk of cornbread. The ordinary bed was a mat on the floor of a room filled with women and children, all of them on mats on the floor.

I wonder what the deluxe bed is, Keeley thought. She thought about changing into her night-clothes, but there were boys in the room, and she didn't want to change in front of them. She stretched out on the mat in her clothes, glad to be safe and out of trouble, at least for the night.

Nearby, a mother held a little girl in her arms, rocking and singing a lullaby. Keeley started missing everyone she had ever loved. She turned away and closed her eyes. Even though she was very tired, it took her a long time to get to sleep.

CHAPTER N.º 5

Winnipeg Free Press
Serbian King and Queen
Assassinated

Breakfast was oatmeal and leftover cornbread.
The oatmeal was lumpier than Mrs. Greer's, but
it was hot, and there was molasses and cream to
put on it. Keeley had had enough experience
with breakfast to know that oatmeal, even with
lumps, would keep her from getting hungry
before the morning was over. She tucked her
piece of cornbread away; it would do for lunch.

No one said goodbye to her as she left the house
with her things. Still, it had been a warm place to
sleep. Keeley tried to memorize the neighbour-
hood in case she had to go back there again.

It was harder to find places in the city. One street looked a lot like another. Frank was so much smaller than Winnipeg. In Frank, it was impossible to lose her way: the mountain was either ahead of her or behind her. The Oldman River was either on her right or on her left.

That, of course, had been before the mountain slide. Now Turtle Mountain was spilled all over the valley, and the Oldman River had turned into a lake.

Keeley brought her mind back to Winnipeg.

"I have to find Cora Hind," she said out loud. Winnipeg was big, but it didn't go on forever. There had to be some way to find her reporter friend.

"The newspaper must have an office." Keeley talked to herself as she walked. She didn't care if people heard her or thought she was strange. If talking to herself helped her to be calm and think straight, then that's what she'd do.

"The Frank *Sentinel* has an office," she continued. "Reporters have to have a place to write their stories, and there has to be a place to keep the printing press and the rows of type. So first I need to find the newspaper office. Then I'll find Cora Hind."

Keeley was quite cheered up by this thought. Finding an office would be easier than finding a person.

She wished she'd thought to ask at the boarding house. She thought of going back, but she was a little scared of the raspy voice and the gnarled hand.

The best thing to do would be to ask a policeman. "I can't do that, though," Keeley said. "They'll put me in jail and send me back to Lethbridge."

She tried to ask people on the street.

"Excuse me," she asked a man unloading a block of ice off a wagon, "do you know where the newspaper office is?"

"Little girl, unless I deliver ice there, I don't know where anything is. Do you think I have time to wander around finding out where places are? Hey, Danny," he called to his helper, "this girl thinks we have time to wander around, finding out where places are."

It's not that *funny,* Keeley thought, walking away as the men laughed at their joke.

"Excuse me," she tried again. People just hurried by.

"Pardon me." Keeley put out her hand to slow down a well-dressed woman who seemed to be in a hurry. "I want to know—"

The woman made *tch, tch* noises, dug into her little drawstring purse, and put a coin into Keeley's hand.

"Thank you," said Keeley, surprised, "but I want—"

"You want more? How ungrateful! I should just take that penny back."

Keeley snatched her hand away. She glared back at the woman. There was no one around to reprimand her, so she was going to be as rude as she wanted to be.

"There ought to be something done," the woman said as she hurried away.

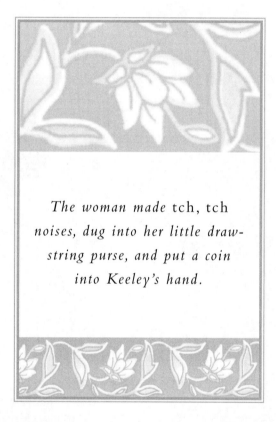

The woman made tch, tch
noises, dug into her little draw-
string purse, and put a coin
into Keeley's hand.

A few people did stop for Keeley, but they didn't know where the newspaper office was. A man and a woman, walking together, each thought the office was in a different direction. They got into a big argument. It was a lot of fun for Keeley to watch, but she didn't learn anything.

She had her lunch on the riverbank, where people had built shacks overlooking the water. Keeley ate her cornbread as slowly as she could. She thought about getting a drink of water from the river but saw some women doing their washing in it and decided she wouldn't bother.

After her lunch, Keeley started walking again, away from the river. The buildings got bigger, and the roads were busier. Carts, horses, and people were all moving in a hurry.

"Paper! Get your paper!" Keeley heard someone call out. "Serbian king and queen assassinated! Read all about it!"

Keeley looked around for the source of the noise, and found it. A boy a few years older than her was standing on the street corner, calling for people to buy his newspapers.

Keeley ran over to him.

"Do you know where the newspaper office is?"

"Of course I do," he said. "Do I look like an idiot?"

"No, you look like just another of the world's many rude boys," Keeley said, folding her arms and planting herself in front of him. "I need to know where the office is."

"And I need to sell these papers." He stepped around her and called out, "Papers here!"

Keeley watched him for a few minutes. He didn't have any customers. "You're not very good at this," she said.

"What do you know?"

"I know I could do a better job than you."

"Don't be stupid," he sneered. "Girls can't sell papers."

"You're just afraid that I'm right." Keeley had an idea. "Give me half your newspapers. If I sell my half before you sell yours, you tell me where the newspaper office is."

"And if I sell my half first?"

"You'll still get them sold faster, so what have you got to lose, except your pride?"

The boy hesitated a moment, then counted out half his papers and handed them to Keeley. "Go down the street a little ways. And keep one foot on your bundle. Folks around here are desperate enough to steal anything."

Keeley put the newspapers under her arm and hurried to the other end of the block. "Get your papers here," she shouted. It came out as a squeak.

This would not do. She pretended she was calling Patricia, way down at the other end of the main street in Frank. She really put some air behind it.

"Get your papers here!"

That was a little too loud. A startled baby began crying, and Keeley got a dirty look from its mother.

"All right, now I know," she said, not so loudly.

The June sun was hot. Keeley took her jacket off, put it on top of her bundle, and kept one foot on top of both of them. She was so grubby anyway, a bit of dust on her clothes would make no difference.

Holding the papers out in front of her, she read the headlines and called out to customers.

"Read all about it! Five thousand hotel workers on strike in Chicago!"

The first time someone pressed money into her hand and took a newspaper, she was so thrilled she did a bit of a dance. This led her smack into the next customer. After that she just concentrated on yelling and selling until there were no newspapers left.

She ran back to the boy. He still had two newspapers left.

"I win!" she said. She turned over the money to him. "Now you have to tell me where the newspaper office is."

The boy put the coins in his pocket. "Look behind you."

Keeley was puzzled for a moment, then looked behind her. The sign on the building said *Winnipeg Free Press*.

She didn't look at the boy's face because she knew he'd be smirking. "I still beat you," she said, then she ran up the steps and into the building.

CHAPTER N.º 6

Keeley was not prepared for the Winnipeg Free Press.

The Frank *Sentinel* operated out of a tiny store on the main street. It was run by one man, Mr. Matheson. He was the owner, publisher, editor, and sole reporter. The only other person who worked there was Keeley, on Saturday mornings. She checked Mr. Matheson's spelling because she was a good speller and he was a lousy one. And during that terrible time after the mountain came down, Keeley worked there as a reporter, errand-runner, and office-sweeper.

Other than that, it was a one-person operation.

The *Winnipeg Free Press* was not.

It was a many-storeyed building, with so many people rushing about that Keeley flattened herself against a wall to avoid getting trampled.

The first big room inside the door had a high counter with a woman sitting behind it. People rushed in, asked the woman a question or dropped something off, then rushed out again.

Keeley waited until there was a lull in the rushing. She needed that time to gather her nerves.

I've come this far, she thought, *I can't back out now*.

She went up to the desk. "I'd like to see Cora Hind, please," she said in a loud, clear voice.

"Newsroom," was the reply.

Keeley took a few steps away, then returned.

"Where is the newsroom?" she asked.

"Up those stairs."

The woman pointed at a door. Keeley went through it, climbed the stairs, and wondered what she'd say.

It was one thing to imagine Cora Hind getting her a job at the newspaper, and the two of them being reporters together. It was another thing to make it happen in reality.

A door off the stairs had a sign saying "Newsroom." Keeley pulled it open.

People talking, typewriters clacking, more rushing back and forth! Keeley was transfixed. Imagine being one of those people! Imagine knowing what to do, and doing it, and then trying to do it better than anybody else had ever done it! Keeley could have watched and listened all day.

"What do you want, kid? Hey—who let this kid in here?" A burly man in shirtsleeves and necktie was towering over her and frowning down at her.

"I … I …," Keeley stammered.

"Come on, out with it! I haven't got all day. I've got a newspaper to put out!"

"I'm looking for Cora Hind," Keeley managed to say.

"Is Miss Hind here?" he bellowed. "Tell her some kid wants her!"

He left Keeley, sat behind a big desk with the sign "Editor" on it. He snatched a piece of paper from a nervous-looking young man and read it with a frown.

Keeley waited. And waited.

Maybe she's not here, she thought. She considered asking the big man with the big frown, but he was busy marking up the nervous man's paper.

Keeley waded into the sea of desks, looking for Cora. She didn't see any familiar faces.

"Hey! What's that kid doing in here?" The bellowing man was at it again.

Keeley had had enough. In a few quick steps, she was at his desk, shoving the nervous guy out of the way.

"My name is Keeley O'Brien, and I'm looking for Cora Hind."

"Didn't I deal with you already?"

"You made a lot of noise, but nothing happened."

Behind her, the newsroom became stone cold silent.

The editor pushed back his chair and rose slowly, his frown getting bigger as his head got higher.

Keeley frowned right back at him. She was too tired to be frightened.

"Where is Miss Hind?" he barked out.

"She's not here," said the young man.

"Then I need to know where she lives," Keeley stated.

"She has an apartment a few blocks away," the young man told her.

"I need to know exactly," Keeley said. She wasn't about to go wandering around the city again.

"I wish my reporters were as tenacious as you," the editor said. "You can read, can't you?"

"And write," Keeley said, wondering what *tenacious* meant.

The young man handed her a piece of paper with Cora's address on it, and explained to Keeley how to get there.

"Now, is there anything else I can do for you today?" the editor asked, with exaggerated courtesy.

Keeley wondered if this would be the right time to ask him for a job. Maybe it would be better to wait until Cora Hind was with her. "Thank you," she said. "That's all for now."

As she left the newsroom, she heard the editor bellow, "Are we running a newspaper or a nursery? Get back to work!"

That will be me he's yelling at soon, Keeley thought happily as she ran down the stairs and out of the building. Cora Hind was waiting.

CHAPTER N.º 7

The nervous young man's directions were easy to follow. Keeley found Cora Hind's apartment on the top floor of a three-storey brick house. She knew she had the right place because there was a small sign on the door that read "C. Hind."

Keeley knocked, but there was no answer.

"I'll just wait here for her," Keeley said. She spoke out loud to give herself courage. The hallway was dimly lit.

She sat on the step and leaned against the door. It had been a long day, and she was tired.

I'm always falling asleep, she thought, just before she fell asleep.

"The door is unlocked," Keeley heard a voice say. She opened her eyes. A cheerful-looking young woman was coming up the stairs. "You could have gone right in."

"You're not Cora Hind," Keeley said.

"No, she's out in the fields, writing about farming methods. Farm women work so hard. They need a more public voice."

I just woke up, Keeley thought.

The woman helped Keeley to her feet. "Let's have some tea."

Keeley followed her into the apartment. She hoped there would be some food served along with the tea.

She stopped just inside the door, and took it all in.

Cora Hind lived in a room that made a lot of sense to Keeley. It wasn't fussy, like her grand-mother's parlour. The chairs and settees looked sturdy and comfortable. Shelves lined one wall, with rather too many books on them for Keeley's taste.

Off to the side was a no-fuss kitchen, and in another room Keeley could see a bed.

"How many people live here with you and Cora?" she asked the woman, who was busy getting the tea.

"Oh, I don't live here. I'm part of the Votes for Women campaign, and there are a lot of meetings in the city this week. Cora lives alone."

I'll live alone, Keeley decided. *During the day, I'll have lots of excitement, and at night, no one will bother me.*

In the meantime, there was plenty of room in this apartment for her. She could sleep on the settee and write her stories on the little table now being set with tea things.

"Are your hands clean?" the woman asked.

"None of me is clean," Keeley said. She took off her jacket, found the soap by the sink, rolled up her sleeves, and washed up to her elbows.

They sat down to tea, which Keeley was glad to see included bread, Cheddar cheese, summer sausage, and date cake. They were both hungry and didn't interrupt their eating with foolish conversation.

At last, Keeley was full. The food and the tea gave her some energy back.

"When does Miss Hind get home?" she asked.

"Tomorrow sometime." The woman sat back and looked at her. Keeley realized she had to say something. She thought about lying, but she was too comfortable and too full of food to go to the bother of making something up.

"I've run away," she said. "I'm supposed to go live with my grandparents in Lethbridge, but my life would be over if I lived with them!"

She glared defiantly at the woman across the table, but the woman nodded calmly, as though she understood.

Keeley continued. "I met Miss Hind in Frank—twice—and I want to be a reporter just like her, so I came here. Look!"

She went to her bundle, and pulled out the newspaper with the article in it. "Here," she said. "I'm already a reporter."

The woman took the newspaper, poured herself some more tea, and read the article.

"You're Keeley O'Brien?" she asked. Keeley nodded. "My name's Nellie McClung." They shook hands. "Your parents?"

"My mother died when I was seven. She's buried here in Winnipeg, but I don't know where. She was a painter, and the art gallery here wants to hang her pictures. My father is under the mountain."

Unless he got out, Keeley thought. Maybe while she's been wandering around Winnipeg, he's crawled out from beneath all the rocks. Maybe he's sitting in the boarding house dining room right now, having his supper and waiting for her to come home.

"Why not tell me the whole story?" Nellie asked.

So Keeley told her all about finally getting away from her grandparents and moving to

They sat down to tea, which Keeley was glad to see included bread, Cheddar cheese, summer sausage, and date cake.

Frank with her father, about meeting Cora Hind, about working at the local newspaper, and about the night the mountain fell. Nellie heard about her friend Patricia and the train journey to Winnipeg, even selling newspapers on the street.

"And what are you hoping for from Cora?" she asked at the end.

Keeley hated moments like this. Speaking wishes out loud to adults always made them seem foolish.

"I was hoping we could be reporters together."

Nellie McClung didn't seem to think that was foolish. "Wonderful! There's a lot happening in the world today, and we need smart, strong women to report on it. Does your grandmother know where you are?"

That was sneaky, Keeley thought, *putting a question like that after a burst of enthusiasm.* "No one knows," she admitted.

Nellie looked at the clock. "It's not too late. We'll go now and send her a telegram."

53

"I'm not going back to Lethbridge!"

"Who said anything about going back?" Nellie fetched their jackets from the hooks by the door. "Worry causes heart attacks. You don't want your grandmother to have a heart attack, do you? We'll just let her know you're safe."

Nellie made the whole idea sound so reasonable that Keeley couldn't think of an objection.

Nellie walked with her head high, with long strides, liked she owned the streets. Keeley had to run a little to keep up with her. The telegraph office was just about to close, but Nellie persuaded them to send one more wire.

It seemed only right to Keeley that she pay for it herself. Another fifty cents came out of her spelling bee money. She tried to figure out how much she had left, but mental arithmetic gave her a headache.

Keeley and Nellie walked back to Cora's apartment through the darkening streets. Keeley thought about all the people she had met since leaving Frank.

"Every day, more and more people come into my head," she said.

"Your head will be a very crowded place before you're through," Nellie answered.

A crowded head. Keeley liked that idea. She smiled and stretched her legs so that her stride matched Nellie's.

I own the streets too, she thought.

CHAPTER N.º 8

Keeley woke up to the sun peeking in through the window blinds. Her sleep had been long and deep, and she felt more rested than she had in weeks. The cushions on the floor were comfortable, and she was exactly where she needed to be.

The evening had been wonderful. After sending the telegram, they had come back to the apartment. Keeley had a good wash in the little kitchen, then Nellie helped her wash and brush her hair. It felt so good to be clean after the grubbiness of the train and the boarding house. It felt especially good to have someone taking care of her again. She could certainly look after herself, but it was comforting to not always have to.

She was also in her nightgown, for the first time since leaving Frank. There were good things about sleeping in her clothes—just jump out of bed, and she's ready for the day—but sleeping in her nightgown was much more comfortable.

She and Nellie had had a late supper of bread and cheese, and had talked until long after she usually went to bed. Nellie had so much to say—about women, about voting, about how alcohol ruins families. They had talked about big things, and Keeley had felt big talking about them.

Quietly, Keeley got out of bed and went over to Cora's desk. She couldn't resist sitting down at it, even though she wasn't quite sure she should.

"This is where Cora Hind writes," Keeley whispered. With the tips of her fingers, she softly stroked the desktop. Maybe some of Cora's talent would seep into her that way.

"Good morning," Nellie said, looking in from the kitchen. Keeley snatched her hands away, but

Nellie just laughed. It was a kind laugh, to show she understood, and Keeley didn't feel bad. "Get yourself together. We've got a busy day ahead of us." She went back into the kitchen to finish making breakfast.

Keeley dressed in clean clothes from her bundle and then tidied Cora's living room.

"What are we going to do?" she asked Nellie while they were eating.

"I have some meetings to go to around the city. I'm hoping you'll come with me."

"I'd like that," Keeley said. She *could* wait at the apartment for Cora to get back, but spending the day with Nellie would be more fun.

The first meeting was in a wealthy part of Winnipeg with big houses and many trees. Nellie talked about women's rights in front of a living room full of ladies in nice dresses. Keeley listened for a while, then spent the rest of the time counting the raspberry tarts on the table, and the number of ladies, and figuring out how many raspberry tarts she was likely to get.

"And who might you be, my dear?" asked a grey-haired lady with pearls, who placed herself between Keeley and the tarts when the meeting took a break.

"I'm a friend of Nellie's," Keeley said, hoping she wouldn't have to resort to pushing the lady out of the way.

"Keeley is in Winnipeg to find her mother's paintings," Nellie said, reaching behind the lady and fetching Keeley a tart. Keeley said thanks and ducked away. She wanted to eat in peace.

More meetings followed. One was in the back of a sewing goods shop. Another was in the crowded dormitory where factory girls lived.

Keeley was tired but excited by the time she and Nellie climbed the stairs to Cora's apartment. Their arms were full of groceries they'd bought at the market.

Nellie opened the door, letting Keeley in first.

Cora Hind was sitting at her desk.

For a long moment, Cora stared at Keeley. Then she came out from behind the desk and gave Keeley a big hug.

"I wasn't sure you survived," Cora said. "Too many newspapers said too many different things."

"You remember me?"

"The fastest runner? The best speller? Of course I remember you."

"I didn't do so well in this year's spelling bee," Keeley told her. That was barely two months ago, before the mountain collapsed.

"We all have our off days." She took the groceries from Keeley, greeted Nellie, then sat on the sofa and picked up her knitting.

"I think we could use a cup of tea," Nellie said.

Keeley sat on the edge of a chair, watching Cora knit and wondering what to do.

The tea came. Cora put her knitting away and they all sat at the table.

"We'll have our tea, then we'll talk," Cora said to Keeley.

The two adults talked about the Votes for Women meetings while Keeley tried to choke down a piece of bread and butter. She wasn't entirely sure that Cora was glad to see her.

"Come and sit by me," Cora said after they finished eating. She picked up her knitting again. "This helps me concentrate," she said. "It's also very useful when I interview politicians. It unsettles them, for some reason, and I can sometimes get them to give me a straight answer. And now I need some straight answers from you. Does anyone know you're here?"

"We sent my grandparents a telegram yesterday," Keeley was glad to be able to say.

"The grandparents are her only relatives left," Nellie said. "Her father was killed in the mountain slide."

"Why did you come to see me?" asked Cora.

"I want to be a reporter."

"I see." Cora's knitting needles clicked and clicked.

Keeley got off the settee and fetched the newspaper with her article in it. She showed it to Cora. Cora put down her knitting and read.

"Very good," she said. "I have to interview some homesteaders tomorrow morning. You'll come with me, find yourself a story there, and write it. We'll show it to my editor in the afternoon. How does that sound?"

"I don't think your editor likes me."

"You don't need him to like you. You need him to like your story. He's the one who will give you the job."

"And if I get the job?"

Cora looked at Nellie. "The working girls' dormitories are mostly for factory workers, but that's not an absolute rule, is it?"

"No, I think they'd rent a bed to Keeley."

Keeley remembered the crowded dormitories. "Couldn't I ... live with you?"

"I prefer to live alone," Cora said. "Also, I travel a great deal. You're too young to be left on your own for weeks at a time."

"I'm not too young," Keeley said. She sat up straight. "I'm sixteen."

Not even Keeley believed that one.

CHAPTER № 9

"Here we are," Cora Hind said, bright and early the next morning. They were at the railway station, but on a different side of the station than Keeley had seen before. "Go find your story."

Keeley looked at the jumble of men, women, children, wagons, horse, oxen, and household goods spread out before them.

"What do I do?"

"All of these people are leaving here today to start a new life in a place they've never seen. Many of them have come from far away. They'll be building farms, living in sod houses, and they'll have to face things they can't even imagine now. Each one of them has a story. Go find one you want to write about."

Cora left Keeley alone then. She had her own story to find.

Keeley didn't know where to start. She had a pencil and a writing tablet with her, but she wasn't sure what to do with them.

I can't just stand here, she thought. *I can't tell Cora that I can't do this.*

Keeley took a deep breath, tightened her grip on her notebook, and started walking into the crowd.

Wagons were pulled up close to the railway tracks. Men were hopping on and off flat-topped railway cars piled high with bundles and crates, to move things from the train to the wagons.

Everyone was busy. Women organized livestock. The bigger children looked after the smaller children. Men carried things and conferred with each other. Some chickens escaped from a crate, and three small boys went chasing after them.

Keeley wandered among all of them. She became so fascinated that she forgot to be nervous.

"Where are you going?" she asked a boy her age who was leading some goats on ropes.

"My family's wagon is up ahead," the boy said.

"No, I mean, where are you going after you leave Winnipeg?"

"Same place you're going. What kind of a question is that?"

One of the goats bumped Keeley where she had sat down.

"Hey! Stop that!" When she turned to scold one goat, another wound itself around her.

"You're messing them up," the boy accused. "Stop it."

"I'm not doing anything. It's them!" One of the goats started chewing on her writing paper. She snatched it away and held it up in the air.

Her screeches made the goats more confused, and their confusion meant Keeley got even more tangled up in their ropes. Her struggle to get free only made things worse.

"Having trouble, little girl?" a man asked, looking down at the scene from the back of a wagon.

Keeley was too busy trying to untangle the goats to answer.

"Stop thrashing around!" the boy said. "You're bothering them."

"*I'm* bothering *them*?" Keeley shouted.

She heard laughter and looked up. A crowd had gathered. Keeley hoped Cora wasn't among them.

"Jonathan! What are you doing?" A tall woman hurried up to them. "There's work to be done."

"I'm not doing anything," Jonathan, the goat boy, said. "She's doing it."

"It looks to me like the goats are doing it." The woman bent down, and in a few short seconds she had the goats sorted out. A handful of people in the crowd applauded. The woman laughed and waved them away.

"Where are your people?" she asked Keeley.

"That's a long story," Keeley said. "Where are you going?"

"Into the unknown," the woman said. She put her arm around the boy's shoulder. "But we'll make it work, won't we, son?"

"Sure we will," Jonathan replied.

"Here we are," the woman said, stopping by a wagon loaded down with furniture and bundles. She tied up the goats, which started munching on clumps of grass. Keeley kept out of their reach.

"Better make sure those bundles are secure," the woman said. "We have a long way to go."

Jonathan jumped onto the wagon.

"How do you know you'll make it work?" Keeley asked her. "You don't know where you're going."

But the woman had gone on to other chores. Keeley tried the boy again.

"Would you be my story?"

"Would I what? You're strange."

"I'm not strange. I'm a reporter. Well, I'm trying to be. If I write this story, I might get the job."

"You're trying to get a job?" That got Jonathan's attention. "I know all about looking for a job." He wound a rope around a bundle.

"Maybe you're not so strange. Help me load the goats, and I'll be your story."

"Load the goats?"

"Sure. You don't expect them to walk, do you?"

I want to be a reporter, Keeley reminded herself. "No problem," she said. "What do I do?"

Keeley helped Jonathan lift the squirming goats onto the wagon and tied them so that they wouldn't fall off or chew anything they weren't supposed to.

Jonathan talked about his life.

"My father was killed in South Africa," he began.

"In the Boer War?" Keeley asked. She knew a bit about that war.

"Are you going to interrupt me all the time?"

I just asked one question, Keeley thought, but she kept quiet.

Jonathan talked about having to leave school in Hamilton, Ontario, about not being able to find work, about his mother's love of farming. They

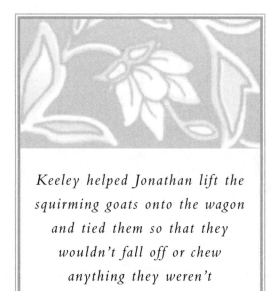

Keeley helped Jonathan lift the squirming goats onto the wagon and tied them so that they wouldn't fall off or chew anything they weren't supposed to.

had a bit of land on the prairie that they'd never seen, and they were going to make a new life there.

The more Jonathan talked, the more Keeley wanted to know. She let him talk for a while so that he didn't mind her questions. Once the goats were on the wagon, she scribbled down his answers on her writing tablet.

His mother returned. "Good job, Jonathan," she said, seeing all the work done.

"She helped," Jonathan said. "She's trying to be a reporter."

"Trying is the only way to make something happen," his mother said.

Keeley had something else she wanted to know. "Are you scared?" she asked them both.

Jonathan and his mother looked at each other. They both nodded.

"But you're going anyway?"

They both grinned. "We sure are."

The other wagons started moving.

"Good luck with your story," Jonathan called out as they waved goodbye.

"Good luck with everything," Keeley replied. She moved to the side of the tracks, out of the way of the procession of carts and wagons.

What will happen to them? she wondered. She should have asked them to write her a letter once they got settled. But where would they send it? All she could do was wish them well.

More people in my head, she thought. Then she ran off to find Cora.

"I've got to go to the office," Cora said after lunch. "Write up your story. Make it two hundred words long. Bring it to the newsroom when you're done. We'll show it to the editor."

They were back in Cora's apartment. Nellie was out, probably at more Votes for Women meetings.

"Make it neat," Cora reminded Keeley. "He has to be able to read it."

Cora left, shutting the door behind her. Keeley was left alone.

She sat down at Cora's desk, took a fresh sheet of paper out of the drawer, straightened her pages of notes, and got ready to work.

Two hundred words. That was all she needed.

She already had a title: "Into the Unknown." She wrote it at the top of the page, and drew a line underneath it. Three words. One hundred and ninety-seven to go.

It was harder than she imagined it would be. She wrote words, then crossed them out again. Whole paragraphs made no sense when she read them over. By the time she'd written two hundred usable words, the pages were a mess of scribbles and lines.

Finally, using her best printing, Keeley made a neat copy of her article. She folded it carefully and left for the newspaper office.

Whatever was going to happen next in her life, it was going to happen now.

CHAPTER N.º 10

"Who let this kid in here?"

Here we go again, thought Keeley.

"My name is Keeley O'Brien. I'm here to see Cora Hind."

The editor frowned, then remembered. "Oh, it's the tenacious one. Well, you can't see Cora Hind right now. She's writing a story for me, and she's on a deadline."

"I've met your deadline." Cora, coming up behind Keeley, dropped some papers on the editor's desk.

"It had better be good," he growled.

"It is." Cora gave Keeley a nudge.

Now was the time.

"Here's *my* story," Keeley said, holding out her neatly printed article. "I'd like a job."

"You want what?"

"I want a job. I want to be a reporter."

"Did you put her up to this?" He glared at Cora.

"Keeley came here from Frank. She helped out at the newspaper there. The least you can do is read her article."

"You're from Frank, kid?" He picked up her article and read it quickly. When he was done, he laid it flat on the desk and picked up his red pencil. In seconds, Keeley's beautifully copied article was covered with red marks. "No lead, no quotes, no last names. I can't tell from this who's supposed to be brave—the goats? It's a mess."

He handed it back to her.

"The answer is no, kid. No job. Not here. Not now."

I'm not going to cry, Keeley thought.

"My answer would be no even if the article was great. When Miss Hind came to me for a job, I told her the newsroom was no place for a woman. I was wrong. Miss Hind is stubborn and aggravating, but she's also a fine reporter. I'll hire more women. But you're not a woman. You're a child. Go home. Go back to school. Grow up. If you still want this when you're older, come and see me. You're on your way. You're just not there yet."

Keeley held her tears until she and Cora were outside the newspaper office. Cora didn't try to comfort her. She didn't say that Keeley should have expected this, or that Keeley could try again when she's older. She let Keeley cry, and, with a gentle touch on her back, steered her through the Winnipeg streets to the safety of the apartment.

Nellie was there when they returned, and dinner was almost ready. Cora and Nellie talked about the Votes for Women meetings. Keeley tried not to think at all.

When the kitchen was clean, Cora asked Keeley to pull a chair up to her desk. "Let's go over your story. Bring me your notes, too."

They talked for two hours. Keeley learned about leads and quotes and how to structure a paragraph.

"What is the heart of this story for you?" Cora asked.

Keeley thought back to her time with Jonathan and his mother. She remembered them driving their wagon away, into the unknown.

"They were scared," Keeley answered, "but they still went."

"Then that should be your lead."

Keeley rewrote her article. She understood what Cora was teaching her. As she wrote, she could feel her mind get bigger. When she was finished, Cora typed it on her typewriting machine.

"It looks professional," Keeley said.

"It reads like a professional story," Cora told her. "Well done."

"I still didn't get the job."

"No, you didn't. But you will be a reporter. Maybe you'll work at the *Winnipeg Free Press*. Maybe you'll work at another newspaper. You could even be a foreign correspondent and travel to other countries."

All of those things sounded very good to Keeley. "But I really wanted to work here," she said. "Now. With you."

"You'll need a different plan."

Keeley nodded. She didn't mind the sound of that. "I need a different plan" was a better way of thinking than "I failed."

"What would you like to do now?" Nellie asked her.

Keeley wasn't quite ready to decide. "Can I let you know in the morning?"

"The morning is a good time to make decisions," Cora agreed.

They made cocoa, and Nellie taught them a new Votes for Women song. Keeley sang, and listened to her friends talk, and thought about what she wanted to do.

In the morning, she was sure.

"I want to go back to Frank," she said. "I want to live with my friend Patricia and her grandmothers. I want to go back to school, and work at the newspaper on Saturdays, and be close to where I lost my father."

Cora believed in acting quickly. "I'll send a telegram to your grandmother. Like it or not, Keeley, she and your grandfather have the right to decide where you live. I'll also send a wire to Patricia's grandmothers. Then we'll see."

Keeley surprised herself by not worrying. She felt ready for whatever was to happen next. If she had to live with her grandparents, she would. She wouldn't run away again. She'd go to school in Lethbridge, and try to get some sort of part-time job at the newspaper there. Even without her friends, she'd be all right.

As they waited for a reply, Nellie kept Keeley busy. "They could use some help at the orphanage," she said. Keeley spent three days spooning cereal into babies and playing with toddlers.

I'm an orphan, too, she realized. She felt very, very lucky to have people who loved her. Her grandparents would take good care of her, even if they didn't understand her.

Her grandmother's telegram came first. It read: "WE LOVE YOU. BE HAPPY. LIVE IN FRANK. KEEP IN TOUCH."

The telegram from Frank came the next day. It had just two words:

"COME HOME."

"I guess there's nothing to do now but go back to Frank," Keeley said. She wondered if she had enough money for her train ticket. She didn't think she'd get away with sneaking on a second time.

"Not quite yet," Nellie said. "We have a surprise for you: we've found your mother's paintings."

City Hall was all lit up.

It looked the way Keeley felt, standing with Nellie and Cora, watching people in fancy clothes look at her mother's paintings.

"The evening is a tremendous success," a woman with grey hair and pearls said to Keeley. This was the same woman who had stood between Keeley and the raspberry tarts at the Votes for Women meeting. She was also the president of the Winnipeg Arts Society.

"She's the one who tracked down the paintings," Nellie had told Keeley earlier.

"We are still a few years away from being able to open our art gallery," the pearl lady said, "but with events like this, Winnipeg will soon become known as the cultural centre of Canada."

Keeley had no idea what the pearl lady was talking about, but it didn't matter. Her mother's paintings looked wonderful on the City Hall walls. She heard the kind words everyone said about them, as they went from painting to painting.

"And this is the daughter? How lovely!" People Keeley didn't know bent down to shake her hand. She smiled back and gave everyone a Votes for Women leaflet. Some of the people believed in women having the vote, and they smiled even more broadly. Some people did not believe in it. Keeley enjoyed watching their faces shift between approval and disapproval.

Some people asked her for her memories of her mother. Keeley didn't want to share them.

They were hers, and she didn't know these people. The first two times she got those questions, she just shrugged in reply. After that, Nellie or Cora would jump into the conversation and move it on to other topics.

"Your mother's paintings are going to be famous," Cora told Keeley. "That means people will want to know about her. You might want to think of a way to tell her story."

"I'll do that," Keeley said.

Somebody made a speech, calling Keeley's mother "an important, original Canadian artist." There was a lot of applause. Keeley ate her supper that evening standing up, taking food off trays carried by waiters.

"If it's all right with you, Keeley, the paintings will stay in Winnipeg for now," Cora said. "I'll act as guardian of them, so that you'll always know where they are."

"Can I have them back some day?"

"You can have them back whenever you want. They're yours. They are worth a lot of money now, and will be worth even more later. That's the way it is with paintings. You might want to sell them later on, and go to university."

The paintings were part of Keeley's mother. Keeley couldn't imagine selling them for any reason, but she understood what Cora was saying.

They stayed at City Hall until all the guests had left. Keeley stood by herself in front of each painting. Sometimes she remembered her mother painting it. Sometimes she thought about how the paintings looked when they hung on the wall of her bedroom at the boarding house in Frank. Sometimes she just remembered her mother.

"You would have loved being here tonight, Mama," she whispered.

The next morning, Keeley left for Frank.

Cora bought her a train ticket. Nellie packed her a bag of snacks to eat on the trip, and gave her Votes for Women leaflets to hand out in Frank.

They both went with her to the train station.

"This isn't goodbye," Nellie said, giving her a hug. "We're in your head now—there's no getting rid of us. Grow up smart and strong. There's work to be done."

"We'll meet again," Cora said. "Remember—I expect great things from you."

Keeley got on the train. She stored her bundle and took a seat beside a young woman. She waved out the window as the train pulled away.

Nellie and Cora would leave the station and go back to their work. They had lots of other people in their lives and lots of other things to think about. Keeley wondered if they would miss her, and felt a little regret that she wasn't staying behind with them.

Keeley watched Winnipeg pass by the train window. As the train moved out onto the prairie, she thought about what was waiting for her—Patricia and her strange but wonderful grandmothers, the tiny office of the Frank

Sentinel and an editor she could learn from, the streets and pathways she'd walked along with her father, and the glorious mountains of the Crowsnest Pass.

"Where are you going?" the young woman asked her.

Keeley answered. "I'm going home."

Dear Reader,

This has been the fourth and final book about Keeley. We hope you've enjoyed meeting and getting to know her as much as we have enjoyed bringing her—and her wonderful story—to you.

Although Keeley's tale is told, there are still eleven more terrific girls to read about, whose exciting adventures take place in Canada's past—girls just like you. So do keep on reading!

And please—don't forget to keep in touch! We love receiving your incredible letters telling us about your favourite stories and which girls you like best. And thank you for telling us about the stories you would like to read! There are so many remarkable stories in Canadian history. It seems that wherever we live, great stories live too, in our towns and cities, on our rivers and mountains. We hope that Our Canadian Girl *captures the richness of that past.*

Sincerely,
Barbara Berson
Editor

1608
Samuel de
Champlain
establishes
the first
fortified
trading post
at Quebec.

1759
The British
defeat the
French in
the Battle
of the
Plains of
Abraham.

1812
The United
States
declares war
against
Canada.

1845
The expedition of
Sir John Franklin
to the Arctic ends
when the ship is
frozen in the pack
ice; the fate of its
crew remains a
mystery.

1869
Louis Riel
leads his
Métis
followers in
the Red
River
Rebellion.

1871
British
Columbia
joins
Canada.

1755
The British
expel the
entire French
population
of Acadia
(today's
Maritime
provinces),
sending
them into
exile.

1776
The 13
Colonies
revolt
against
Britain, and
the Loyalists
flee to
Canada.

1837
Calling for
responsible
government, the
Patriotes, following
Louis-Joseph
Papineau, rebel in
Lower Canada;
William Lyon
Mackenzie leads the
uprising in Upper
Canada.

1867
New
Brunswick,
Nova Scotia
and the United
Province of
Canada come
together in
Confederation
to form the
Dominion of
Canada.

1870
Manitoba joins
Canada. The
Northwest
Territories
become an
official
territory of
Canada.

1784
Rachel

Timeline

1885
At Craigellachie, British Columbia, the last spike is driven to complete the building of the Canadian Pacific Railway.

1898
The Yukon Territory becomes an official territory of Canada.

1914
Britain declares war on Germany, and Canada, because of its ties to Britain, is at war too.

1918
As a result of the Wartime Elections Act, the women of Canada are given the right to vote in federal elections.

1945
World War II ends conclusively with the dropping of atomic bombs on Hiroshima and Nagasaki.

1873
Prince Edward Island joins Canada.

1896
Gold is discovered on Bonanza Creek, a tributary of the Klondike River.

1905
Alberta and Saskatchewan join Canada.

1917
In the Halifax harbour, two ships collide, causing an explosion that leaves more than 1,600 dead and 9,000 injured.

1939
Canada declares war on Germany seven days after war is declared by Britain and France.

1949
Newfoundland, under the leadership of Joey Smallwood, joins Canada.

1903
Keeley

1885
Marie-Claire

1915
Millie